*

To the
best gifts of all —
John, Timothy, & Noelle

First edition 2000

Library of Congress Cataloging-in-Publication Data
Kvasnosky, Laura McGee.
Zelda and Ivy One Christmas / Laura McGee Kvasnosky—1st ed.
p. cm.
Summary: After making a special Christmas gift for their elderly
neighbor, two sisters find just what they wanted under their tree.
ISBN 0-7636-1000-3
[1. Foxes—Fiction. 2. Sisters—Fiction. 3. Christmas—Fiction.
4. Neighbors—Fiction.] I. Title.
PZ7.K975 Zek   2000
[Fic]—dc21   99-046810

2 4 6 8 10 9 7 5 3 1

Printed in Italy

This book was typeset in Myriad Tilt.
The illustrations were done in gouache resist.

Candlewick Press
2067 Massachusetts Avenue
Cambridge, Massachusetts 02140

Zelda and Ivy
ONE CHRISTMAS

LAURA McGEE KVASNOSKY

CANDLEWICK PRESS
CAMBRIDGE, MASSACHUSETTS

Chapter One

CHRISTMAS WISHES

One frosty morning, Zelda and Ivy helped their neighbor Mrs. Brownlie bake gingerbread cookies.

"Christmas is almost here," said Mrs. Brownlie. "What do you hope Santa will bring?"

"A Princess Mimi doll," said Ivy quickly. "With the pink tutu and all the ballet accessories."

Zelda scratched her head. "I'm still deciding," she said.

   While the cookies were baking, Mrs. Brownlie took out a
Christmas catalog. "Maybe this will help," she said.
   Zelda pawed through the catalog, past the toys, past the
furniture. When she came to evening wear, she stopped.
   "Voilà," she said.

"That," said Mrs. Brownlie, "is a very snazzy bracelet."

"Not the bracelet," said Zelda. "I want the dreamy velvet gown." She lifted her muzzle. "Perfect for a Christmas Ball."

"But you've never been to a Christmas Ball," said Ivy.

"I haven't had the right dress," said Zelda.

"The last time Mr. B. and I danced was at a Christmas Ball," said Mrs. Brownlie. She pointed to a photograph. "We waltzed and whirled like snowflakes."

"Mr. B. was a good dancer," said Ivy. "Remember last year when he taught us the Tinsel Town Hop?"

Mrs. Brownlie smiled, remembering. "Christmas is not the same without him."

"I miss him, too," said Ivy.

Zelda nodded. For once, she didn't know what to say.

Later, Zelda and Ivy sloshed home in the snow.

"I think I'll make Mrs. Brownlie a present," said Ivy. "To cheer up her Christmas."

"That's just what I was thinking," said Zelda.

"Like a bracelet," said Ivy.

"That's just what I was planning, too," said Zelda.

Ivy pulled out the craft box. "I'll string the beads," she said.

"No," said Zelda. "You get the glitter ready."

"I'll sprinkle the glitter," said Ivy.

"No," said Zelda. "You get the wrapping paper."
"At least let me wrap it," said Ivy. "It *was* my idea."
"Well, okay," said Zelda. "You can hold the knot while I tie the bow."

Zelda wrote the card in her best cursive:
To Mrs. B. from her Christmas Elves
"Voilà," she said.

"Let's put it under our tree until Christmas," said Ivy.
"I was just going to do that," said Zelda. "But you can
if you really want to."

Later, when Ivy wasn't looking,
Zelda moved the present close to
her favorite ornament.

Chapter Two

CHRISTMAS FORTUNES

Zelda balanced a golden Christmas
ornament on the birdbath and wrapped
her muffler around her head like a turban.
"I am the Amazing Zeldarina," she said.
"I can read the future in this magic ball."
"Okay," said Ivy. "What will Santa bring
me for Christmas?"

Zelda looked into the ball. "I see a fox. Tall, orange, and handsome. You will marry him and have three babies named Bobo, Walter, and Polly."

"Come on," said Ivy. "Tell me about Christmas."
"You will journey far, to Zanzibar and Zamboanga,"
answered Zelda.

"Oh boy," said Ivy. "But will Santa Claus bring me a Princess Mimi doll with the pink tutu and all the ballet accessories?"

Zelda looked thoughtful. "I see a glimmer of a velvet gown," she said.

"That's probably for you," said Ivy.

"Of course," said Zelda. She lifted her muzzle. "For the Christmas Ball."

"Do you see anything for me?" asked Ivy.

Zelda leaned in close. Just then the sweet smell of apple pie drifted up the street.

"Sorry," she said, as she followed the scent toward Mrs. Brownlie's. "Your time is up. The Amazing Zeldarina has spoken."

Ivy stood and looked deeply into the
ornament. She thought—she really
thought—she saw a Princess Mimi doll.

Chapter Three

CHRISTMAS GIFTS

"Let's pretend we're sisters," said Ivy.

"We are sisters," said Zelda.

"I know, but it's more fun to pretend," said Ivy. "And let's pretend we are lying in our beds on Christmas Eve, waiting for Santa."

"We are," said Zelda, yawning.

"And let's pretend Santa Claus brings me a Princess Mimi doll," said Ivy.

"Oh, all right," said Zelda. "As long as we pretend he brings me an evening gown."

Ivy was almost asleep when Zelda nudged her. "Go see what Santa left," she whispered.

"We can't go downstairs," said Ivy. "Not until morning."

"Come on," said Zelda. "Pretend to tiptoe down and look." She handed Ivy her slippers.

"Well, okay," said Ivy. "But I'm just pretending."

When Ivy came back, she looked sad. "Santa hasn't come," she sniffed. "The cookies we put out are still there."

"It must be too early," said Zelda. "Let's go back to sleep."

"I can't sleep," said Ivy.

"Pretend," said Zelda.

Christmas morning, two big boxes from Santa Claus were next to the tree. Boxes big enough to hold an evening gown or a Princess Mimi doll. Zelda and Ivy opened them eagerly to find . . . matching bathrobes.

"This robe is pure glamour," said Zelda. She put it on
and tried to pose like the model in Mrs. B.'s catalog.
But it wasn't the same.

Then Ivy noticed two more big boxes under the tree.

She crawled in for a closer look. "The tags say *To Zelda* and *To Ivy*," she read. "*Love, The Christmas Elf!*"

"Mine first," said Zelda. She tore off the wrapping. "Just what I wanted!" she shouted. Nestled in the tissue was a velvet gown, with gloves and a feather boa.

Next, Ivy carefully untaped the wrapping and slipped off
the lid to her box. "Oh my," she whispered. "Princess Mimi!"

Zelda put on her new gown. "This is exactly like the one
in Mrs. B.'s catalog," she said. "Let's go show her."

"Okay," said Ivy. "We can take her the present we made."

Zelda and Ivy knocked on Mrs. Brownlie's door. When she opened it, lovely Christmas music spilled onto the porch. "What a nice surprise," said Mrs. B. "Come in!"

Zelda handed Mrs. Brownlie the gift. "The Christmas Elves left this under our tree," explained Ivy.

Mrs. Brownlie unwrapped the gift and held the new bracelet up to the light.

"This," she said, "is so snazzy! How did the Christmas Elves know exactly what I wanted?"

Zelda and Ivy grinned.

"A Christmas Elf brought us just what we wanted, too," said Ivy. "See my Princess Mimi?"

"Pleased to meet you, Princess Mimi," said Mrs. B.

"And this is my new gown," said Zelda, twirling.

"That looks like a dancing dress, all right," said Mrs.
Brownlie. She turned up the music, then held out one
paw to Zelda and the other to Ivy.

"Shall we dance?" she asked.

They waltzed and whirled like snowflakes.

"You know," said Ivy. "This is like having our own Christmas Ball."

"That's just what I was thinking," said Zelda.

When the music ended, they all curtsied.

"Merry Christmas," said Zelda and Ivy.

"Yes," said Mrs. Brownlie. "A very merry Christmas!"